Tullio's Orange Tree

A Fable by Ted Gerstl

Illustrated by Jan Albertin

Millennium

An imprint of The Millennium Publishing Group
Distributed to the book trade by Summit Publishing Group

Library of Congress Cataloging-in-Publication Data

Gerstl, Ted 1944—
Tullio's Orange Tree
Internal Illustrations by Albertin, Jan
p. 40cm
ISBN 1-88882-002-0
1. Fiction
2. Fables
3. Italy

II. Title

©1996 by Ted Gerstl
Cover artwork ©1996 by Ruth Sanderson

Typeset by Morris Design, Monterey, California

Printed in Hong Kong
2 4 6 8 9 7 5 3 1

Dedication

For Candy

High atop a hill in the little village of Pieve a Elici stood an old abandoned farmhouse. Although its outside walls remained, the rest of the house was in shambles. The surrounding land was dotted with olive trees, but these, too, were in sorrowful condition brought about by years of neglect.

Rob and his wife, Karen, had come to Italy to try to find an old *rustico* in Tuscany, a house that they could restore and perhaps live in some day. They had been visiting the beautiful eleventh century church, San Pantaleone, when they spotted the old house. Perched on a small hill, its beautiful golden stone walls glistened in the sun. They went around the church, past the old cemetery, and walked down the little road to see the house.

"This was the house of *contadini*," Karen told their eleven year old son, Jesse, "the farmers who tended the olives. This house is hundreds of years old. Just think, Jesse, what stories this old house could tell."

While Karen and Jesse were imagining life in the eighteenth century, Rob wandered off to look at the old house. There were no doors or windows left and everything of value had been removed. It had once been a three-story house, but what used to be the middle floor was missing. The *terracotta* bricks were no longer there. All that remained inside were some old wooden beams and a steep wooden stairway which ascended to the top floor.

Rob carefully walked across the beams and climbed the stairway, finding a room almost untouched by the passing years.

He dusted himself off and walked around on the bricks which were, if uneven and somewhat chipped, in quite good condition. He walked over to the hole in the wall where the window once was and looked out over Lake Massaciuccoli and the Mediterranean Sea. The hills were covered with millions of olive trees and, on the horizon, Rob could see the Leaning Tower of Pisa.

Rob was entranced with the view, the tranquility of the beautiful setting. He listened to the contrasting sounds: the distant hum of the *autostrada* mixed with the sweet chirping of birds; the melodious chiming of church bells interrupted by the buzzing of a chain saw; the sea breezes rushing through the olive trees, punctuated by the distant gunshots of the *cacciatore*, the weekend hunters.

From the lower floor came Karen's voice: "Come look at this floor, Rob." It wasn't really a floor, but a series of wooden beams and rafters that once had supported a floor. "Look at these nails," she said. "These nails were made by hand, probably from Gombitelli," recalling her research of the area.

Gombitelli, a village seven or eight kilometers away, was known in the seventeenth and eighteenth centuries as the center for nail-making.

"Do they still make nails?" Jesse asked.

"I don't think so," Karen responded, "but we can go there and see later on."

There was something enchanting about this house, this land. But why had it been abandoned? Who had lived here? Who owned it now? Was it for sale? As Rob silently pondered these questions, Jesse noticed an old man meandering toward the house.

"*Buongiorno, Signore,*" Rob called out to him. He was walking slowly among the olive trees with the help of an old gnarled stick. Looking up at Rob, he stopped to take off his hat and wipe his brow with a handkerchief.

"*Buongiorno,*" he responded with twinkling eyes and a warm smile. He said his name was Tullio.

Although Rob spoke only a little Italian, he managed to ask the old man about the house at the top of the hill. "Oh, yes, I know it," the old man said, "very well." Tullio had been born in the house, as had his mother, grandmother, and great-grandmother before him. He now lived in the town, but came to the house every now and then, "just to walk among my olive trees." He added a little sadly, "I was born with the olives and I'll die with the olives." His eyes watered with emotion as he reflected, "I love to come here and sit by the old orange tree, remembering..."

His voice trailed off, as if he were sliding into his own reverie. "Remembering what?" Rob thought, but said nothing. It was not the time to intrude.

Tullio looked around his beloved land, at his trees, seeing things that no one else could see. He paused to watch Jesse and Karen walking up the trail to the local *frantoio*, where olives are pressed into oil. Rob watched the old man and noticed the corners of his mouth give way to a smile.

Rob tried to imagine Tullio as a boy his own son's age. "Ahhh," Tullio said, "look at those poor trees." He shook his head and again wiped his brow in contemplation. "It would take three years to bring these trees back to life. I'm an old man now, and I'm afraid I won't see it in my lifetime."

"Of course you will, Tullio," Rob said to reassure him, but looking up at the old house and surveying the land overgrown with brambles, he too had his doubts. As they talked, Tullio started walking around the property, pointing out the borders with his walking stick.

The two men chatted a little longer, and when the time came to say goodbye, Tullio reached out and gently took both of Rob's hands in his. He looked straight into Rob's eyes and said, "Do an old man a favor. Before you leave, spend a moment or two sitting by my orange tree."

My orange tree, Rob noted silently.

"Go sit by my orange tree and look out onto the olive trees. Let yourself..."

Rob did not understand the last few words, but he smiled and nodded and said, "*Ho capito,* I understand," because even though he did not understand all the words, there was no mistaking what was in the old man's eyes, in his grasp, and in his heart.

Tullio turned to walk away.

"*Ciao,* Tullio," Rob yelled as he watched him disappear. "*Ci vediamo,* I'll see you again."

"*Speriamo,*" Tullio shouted back over his shoulder, waving his walking stick, "let's hope."

Rob walked back toward the house, appreciating Tullio's love of this land.

And that's when he saw it for the first time.

Nestled against one of the walls of the old house was the orange tree. But not just an ordinary orange tree. It was magnificent, almost three stories high, and laden with oranges. While everything else around it was dry and overgrown, the orange tree was alive and flourishing. Rob searched for Karen and Jesse, eager to tell them about his conversation with Tullio, but they were nowhere to be found.

He decided to take Tullio's advice and sit down by the orange tree. Rob remembered Tullio's words: "Do an old man a favor..." He reached up and plucked a plump orange—an orange whose sweetness, he thought, would equal the sweet dreams that were beginning to fill his head.

When he sat down, his mind was spinning. What would it be like to restore the old house? To live in Italy? To study and speak Italian? Where would Jesse go to school?

He thought about Tullio, imagining Tullio sitting by the orange tree and remembering...remembering what?

The afternoon sun warmed Rob as the gentle sea breezes conspired with the quiet serenity of the hills. Leaning back against the tree, he closed his eyes and raised his face to the sun. The bells of San Pantaleone chimed three o'clock and Rob felt drowsy. He listened to the chirping birds as they flitted from tree to tree. He could make out the faint sound of olives dropping into the bright orange netting that covered the surrounding hillside. Too sleepy to peel the orange, he put it in his coat pocket, closed his eyes, and let his dreams carry him away...

Chapter Two

Rob had forgotten about the orange until the family got home that evening to their rented house in Viareggio. He took it out of his pocket and placed it on the kitchen table, planning to eat it later. From time to time that evening, he found himself glancing at the large, succulent orange, as it now seemed to symbolize the sweetness of their future in Italy. He smiled at the thought of the orange tree forever filling their bowls with sweet, juicy fruit. He could practically smell the fragrance of orange blossoms filling the garden.

That night, after Karen and Jesse had fallen asleep, Rob remained in the living room and watched the glowing embers in the fireplace. He was thinking about Tullio when he remembered the orange. He walked into the kitchen and picked it up, but hesitated before peeling it. Curiously, he felt sentimental and filled with a growing sense of anticipation. He held the orange up and declared: "Ah, my sweet orange tree, you and I will grow old together. I will care for you and you will reward me with sweet, delicious oranges for all our years."

He couldn't wait any longer. He peeled the orange, tore off a small section, popped it in his mouth and bit down.

"Blechh!" he said, spitting the bitter fruit into the sink. It tasted awful! He had expected his first bite to be sweet and juicy, and was overcome with feelings of disappointment. But more than that, he felt somehow... betrayed. Such strong emotions from just tasting an orange, he thought. Trying to become more rational, he reflected: Perhaps I was too hasty in picking the orange from the tree before it was ripe, or maybe I just picked the wrong orange. Perhaps I got a little carried away with my dreams and expectations.

He grudgingly ate a slice of bread to get rid of the sour taste. He was beginning to have mixed feelings about the old abandoned house, high atop a hill in Pieve a Elici, surrounded by withering olive trees, the one with the beautiful orange tree, the orange tree which offered him bitter fruit.

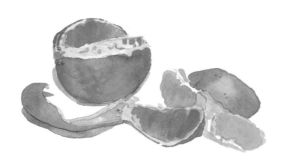

Chapter Three

R ob awoke the next morning refreshed and full of his usual optimism. It's funny how things seem so much more difficult or sinister at night, he thought. He was anxious to take another look at the old house and reawaken his original enthusiam. He made some inquiries about the house and found out that it was for sale. The family packed a picnic lunch (including store-bought oranges), and drove to Pieve a Elici.

They ate lunch at San Pantaleone, sitting on the eleventh century wall. It wasn't long before they began to envision the house fully restored, complete with antiques and a large *terrazza* on which they would have their meals on beautiful sunny days, with sea breezes whispering through the hills. After finishing their lunch, they walked around the church, down an old footpath through the olive trees, back to the house to have another look.

While Karen and Jesse went inside to plan the rooms, Rob walked around to the side of the house. As he turned the corner, he was startled to hear a woman's voice.

"Oh, you're back," the voice grumbled. He instinctively looked for Karen. But when he glanced around to see who was speaking, there was no one.

"Who's that?" said Rob. "Karen, is that you?" There was no answer.

"I said, 'You're back!' What do you want here?" the same voice demanded. He entered the house, looking for the source of the voice, but no one was there. He went back outside and reconstructed the scene in his mind. The voice had seemed to be coming from the direction of the orange tree. Making sure that no one else was around, he walked right up to the tree and said, "Were you talking to me?"

There was no response from the tree, of course, and he felt rather silly. But he noticed a little clump of oranges, appearing perfectly ripe and delicious. This time he was very careful to pick the very best orange. He peeled it and popped a piece into his mouth.

Rob choked. This orange was even more sour and bitter than the first! His lips began to sting as if he had tasted pure acid! Muttering to himself, he threw the rest of the orange as far as he could over the olive trees. And, taking the bitter orange as an omen, he threw away a dream.

Karen and Jesse were busy making plans and designing rooms when he approached them and said, "Let's go. I don't think this is going to work out."

"But why, Dad?" asked Jesse.

"What's the matter, honey?" his wife asked. "What's changed?"

A little embarrassed, Rob tried to cover up the real reasons for wanting to leave. Searching quickly in his mind, he mumbled something about the enormous cost of restoring the house. Such a sudden reversal of plans aroused suspicion in both Karen and Jesse. They didn't say anything more, but Rob saw the disappointment in their eyes and felt terrible. Not knowing what to say, he turned away and started walking down the path toward the car. His lips were stinging and his head was spinning. Karen followed closely behind, hugging Jesse as they approached the car.

While Karen and Jesse shuffled into the car, Rob hesitated a moment and took one last melancholy look at the old house. It was then that he heard the voice once again: "Good riddance!"

And then, just a little sadly, it said, "Don't come back."

Chapter Four

Conversation was subdued at dinner that night. Jesse even offered to wash the dishes rather than watch his favorite Italian television show. Karen and Rob settled in the living room. Not one for letting things slide, Karen asked: "What really happened at the house this afternoon?"

Sometimes, Rob reflected, Karen is a little too perceptive, especially when it comes to my feelings. He began to tell her about the orange tree. He told her about the first bitter orange and the second orange that had stung his mouth. "I don't know why," he said, "but somehow that tree has come to represent all that was sweet and wonderful about our dreams. Now, after tasting those two oranges, I feel...I feel..."

"Betrayed?" Karen offered.

Rob nodded, surprised by both the strength of his emotion and the accuracy of Karen's insight.

"The orange tree seems very special to you," she said softly.

"There's more," he volunteered. He told her about the voice that he heard at the house, but he dared not speculate that it had come from the orange tree. He felt silly telling this to Karen. She just listened and said, "Go back tomorrow. Go by yourself. Try to listen again, but be patient," she cautioned. "There's something quite magical about this place. I just feel it."

Chapter Five

"Talking trees! What kind of nonsense is this?" Rob thought, as he began to cope with the noise and congestion of life in Viareggio. It was market day in the seaside resort, and the traffic was even worse than normal. He drove past the *passagiata,* already packed with people shopping and going to the beach. People were going about their business as usual, but not Rob: he was going to Pieve a Elici to try to communicate with an orange tree!

He decided not to take the *autostrada.* He needed time to think, and driving through the hills would provide him not only time but a transition to a different place, far away from twentieth century Italy. He took the Freddana mountain pass through the Versilian hillside villages, fifteen minutes and two hundred years away from Viareggio. By the time he arrived at the narrow, winding road that led to Pieve a Elici, he felt both a quiet serenity coming over him and a sense of growing excitement and anticipation. He drove past the old *frantoio* and turned down the road that took him to the property. As he approached the house, he stopped the car, got out, and looked at the vistas around him. To his left was the exquisite church tower of San Pantaleone, rising proudly from the green hills. Below were the still waters of Lake Massaciuccoli and the sparkling blue Mediterranean. To his right were the tiny villages of Spesi and Coli with their narrow cobblestone streets and eighteenth century houses. Behind him was the ancient town of Montigiano, poised majestically on a mountaintop and beyond that the snowy, craggy peaks of the Apennines. And everywhere, olive trees.

He walked slowly up the driveway and went around the back to the orange tree. To his amazement, he was greeted with, "You, again?" in a voice a little less gruff than before. "Just what is it you want?"

Rob hesitated, took a deep breath, and began. "Yesterday, you told me not to come back. You sounded so unfriendly. And when I ate your fruit, I was convinced you wanted nothing to do with me and my family."

The orange tree made a noise, its branches swaying slightly. "I felt confused and disappointed," Rob continued, "because I so wanted to be with you. Remember, I came to sit near you?"

He waited for a response, but none came, so he continued: "You asked me what I wanted, so I will tell you. I want to hear your story. I want to know why you were so unfriendly to me, why you wanted to scare me away. I want to know why you make it so hard for people to like you."

He hesitated again, waiting for a reaction. He was afraid of overwhelming the tree, but once he got started, he couldn't stop. "And if you really want to know what I want," he said, deciding to take a risk, "I want to make friends with you. I want to take care of you. Please," he pleaded, "talk to me."

He sat by the tree and waited. He concentrated on his wife's words: "Be patient." And he was rewarded. Was it the rustling of the leaves in the wind, or was she clearing her throat to speak?

The tree spoke, softly and slowly: "Tullio's great-grandparents planted me over one hundred years ago," she said. "They were good people who lived off the land. They planted and harvested the olive trees that surround me. But of all the trees they planted, they put me in the best location—right next to the house, where I could bathe in the sun and feel the warm sea breezes coming up through the valley.

"With every year I grew stronger and sweeter. I watched as Tullio's grandmother came into the world, and after that, his mother. With each generation, I gave freely of my bounty and in return I was loved and nourished.

"But my best years were still to come. Tullio's mother gave birth to eight children, and those years were the most wonderful. If I gave one hundred oranges a year to Tullio's great-grandmother and two hundred oranges a year to Tullio's grandmother, then I gave a thousand oranges each year to Tullio's mother and her children."

Rob listened with rapt attention as the orange tree told her story. He noticed that as she talked about Tullio's parents and his seven brothers and sisters, she pulled herself up to full height. And, even if she seemed a bit boastful or perhaps tended to exaggerate a little, he was beginning to feel differently about the tree. The more she revealed of herself, the more he liked her.

"Oh, if you could have seen me then," she continued. "If you could have sampled my oranges. There were no sweeter, no finer oranges on the face of the Earth. And I'll let you in on a little secret. I saved my sweetest oranges for Tullio.

"All the children loved me, but no one took better care of me than Tullio. During the dry season, he always made sure I had enough to drink. And during the cold, rainy months, he made sure I had the protection I needed. When I needed pruning, he was always careful to do it with the least amount of discomfort to me. Please don't think ill of me when I say that when Tullio trimmed my branches, I was the most beautiful orange tree in all of Pieve a Elici, if not the world."

He listened in silence, occasionally nodding his head as her story unfolded. He interjected only for clarification or to encourage her to keep talking.

His mind was filled with images of Tullio as a boy, and the splendor of the surrounding land. He pictured the family working all day gathering the olives, eating supper around a large table, the fireplace aglow with the slow-burning wood of the olive trees. He pictured the kitchen table overflowing with oranges from the tree, and happy children being tucked into bed, four to a room. He could see the family walking up the hill to church on Sundays. And he saw a young Tullio sitting by the orange tree in the afternoon sun. He envisioned the orange tree embracing the children with her branches, and the children dancing around her.

Rob was enjoying his fantasies when the mood changed suddenly. The sky turned gray and foreboding and the light sea breezes turned cold and threatening.

The orange tree said with finality, "I don't want to say any more."

Rob worried that he had done something to offend her. He wondered what accounted for this sudden change of mood. But once again, Karen's words came to him: "Be patient."

He guessed that the next chapter in her story might be a little difficult for her to talk about, so he said to her, "I think I understand why you don't want to say any more today. I enjoyed our time together. I'm no longer afraid of you, and I hope you're no longer afraid of me."

The tree said nothing.

"I want you to know," Rob continued, "that if you ever want to tell me more, I would be most pleased to listen."

Hearing no response, he stood to leave. He was walking slowly down the driveway when he heard her voice: "Will you return?"

"Will tomorrow be too soon?"

Chapter Six

He was in a haze all the way home. He could not remember starting the car, the winding roads or even the traffic approaching Viareggio. He thought: "What on Earth do I say to Karen and Jesse? I'm a rational man, a practical man. How do I explain to them that I've had a conversation with a talking tree? Maybe I'll keep it a secret. Who would believe it anyway? Maybe this is a dream. Did I make it all up? Yes, yes, that's it—I won't mention a word of this to anyone."

Feeling back in control, Rob calmly opened the front door, walked in, and shouted, "The tree talks! The tree talked to me!"

Unable to contain his excitement, for the next hour he told Karen and Jesse everything that had happened, every word, every feeling. They listened in amazement and wonder.

Jesse's imagination was in high gear. "Are you going back, Dad? You have to go back, Dad. Can I go with you next time, Dad? Please. Oh, *please!*"

"I know it's exciting, honey," Karen told Jesse. "But I'm afraid we're going to have to wait for Dad's next visit to find out more. It seems the orange tree has chosen to tell her story to Dad. We have to be patient."

They talked of nothing else for the rest of the day.

And of course it was difficult for Rob to sleep that night, anxiously anticipating his next encounter with the orange tree, *Tullio's orange tree,* as he was beginning to think of her.

Chapter Seven

Rob arrived at the old house in the middle of the morning. He sat next to the tree, in the very same spot as the day before, and greeted her with *"Buongiorno."* There was no response. Thinking that the tree had not heard him, he repeated his greeting a little louder. Still, there was no response.

Rob said nothing for a long time, in fact for hours. And for hours the tree said nothing to acknowledge his presence. By early afternoon, it was beginning to get hot, so he decided to find a shadier spot for lunch. But as he got up, the tree demanded, "Don't leave!" and then added, a little more softly, "please."

"I wasn't going to leave," he told her. "Just move for a little while as it was getting very hot and..."

"But don't move just yet," she implored. "I was just about to tell you...that is, if you still want to know..." She appeared a little embarrassed that she had been so presumptuous.

"Oh, I do, I do," he said reassuringly. He sat down nearer to the tree and took out his water bottle. He was just about to take a drink, when he turned to the tree and said, "Would you care for a drink of water? You surely must be hot in this sun too."

"How kind of you," she said in a tone he had not heard before.

That afternoon he heard all about the tragedies that had befallen Tullio's family. There were illnesses and untimely deaths. There were feuds between family members—uncles, aunts and cousins, even brothers and sisters—that brought years of conflict and sadness to the house.

And then, when Tullio was only fourteen, hard times fell on the whole world, and Tullio's parents could no longer make a living from the olives. They could not afford to stay in their house. They were forced to abandon their olive trees and, of course, their orange tree.

Years passed. Grandparents and parents died. Children moved away to the cities where they could find work. They married and began to raise their families far away from their old land. Finally, the house deteriorated into a state of ruin. Passersby threw rocks, breaking all the windows. Rains and wind destroyed the inside of the house, even though the old stone walls remained proudly intact. Everything of value in the house was stolen. Weeds took over and choked the olive trees. Everything was affected. But from the orange tree's point of view, she was affected the most.

The tree's voice was softer now, more hesitant and pensive.

"For years after everyone left," she said, "I continued to bear sweet oranges, but no one came to enjoy them. Oh, strangers would wander onto the land and rip an orange from my branches, but I was very lonely. At first I was hopeful that someone would return to take care of me. But no one did. I would go for months without water, and then when the rains came, I would be battered by the winter storms and be left to shiver in the cold. With no one to prune my branches, I began to feel awkward and ugly. No one needed me anymore. And there was no one to eat my sweet oranges."

Rob moved a little closer to the orange tree.

"It was then that I began to change," she said with sorrow in her voice. "Or should I say, that was when changes came over me."

Her branches were beginning to droop. Rob could see that she was entering a very painful part of her story.

"The worst thing that could happen to a living tree happened to me," she disclosed. "I was neglected and abandoned, rejected and unloved. I had become barren. I stopped giving, stopped growing. Everyone had forsaken me," she whispered, "even Tullio."

It was getting late and the sun was beginning to set over Lake Massaciuccoli. Tired from not sleeping well the night before, and exhausted from the day's events, Rob tried to stifle a series of yawns. He was concerned that the tree might think he was bored or disinterested. She must have noticed something because she said rather abruptly, "Perhaps that's enough for today."

Rob pleaded for her to continue, but she remained silent.

"Please," he said, "don't misunderstand. I'm only yawning because I was so excited after our talk yesterday that I couldn't get to sleep. If you allow me, I'll return tomorrow."

She said not another word.

Chapter Eight

All the way back home, Rob reflected on what the tree had told him. The tree had seemed so unfriendly and mean when he first had encountered her, but she was different now. He thought about how sometimes people are so different inside from the way they appear; about how difficult it sometimes is to reach out when one is afraid of getting hurt; about how lonely she must have been all those years.

But mostly, driving home, what he felt was that he was beginning to care for her.

And yet, there were questions: Why did she choose to talk with him? If she was barren, how did she start bearing fruit again? And what about Tullio? She had told him that even Tullio had forsaken her, but he had seen him just a few days before.

He was anxious to see her again, to hear the rest of her story. But what if she no longer wanted to talk? What if he had offended her? What if she closed up again?

All of a sudden, he felt a little scared...and a little vulnerable.

And he realized that it was not only the orange tree who had risked something that day.

Chapter Nine

The next day, the family took a drive to Florence and enjoyed the museums, galleries, and splendor of the city. It was late afternoon before they returned to Viareggio.

Jesse hadn't forgotten the magic tree and, as they were pulling into their driveway, he asked, "Aren't you going to visit the orange tree today, Dad? Can't we come with you?"

"Give me one more day alone with the orange tree, Jesse...please," Rob said, pulling him closer. Rob and Karen glanced at each other and shared an unspoken acknowledgment of Jesse's patience and understanding.

He arrived at the old house almost twenty-four hours to the minute since he had last spoken with the orange tree. He approached the tree with some trepidation, not knowing if she would be happy to see him or angry because he hadn't come sooner. "*Buona sera,* beautiful tree," he said. "I'm sorry I am so late, but my family and I were..."

"Good evening to you, kind sir," the tree said, to Rob's relief. "I am happy to see you."

The sun was setting over Lake Massaciocculi and the silvery green leaves of the olive trees were shimmering in the twilight.

How different she appeared from their first meeting, Rob thought. Unable to contain his growing affection, he said, "When I first met you, you seemed so gruff and unfriendly. You know, I think you tried to chase me away at first. I felt that you used your oranges, your bitter oranges, to keep me from getting close to you."

"I was afraid..." she whispered.

"You were only hurting yourself by pushing me away. What I think you really wanted was to have someone come close to you, to care for you."

"I was afraid..." she repeated.

"I understand. You were abandoned. But that was long ago. It's difficult to trust again."

"I'm trying," she said softly.

"I know."

"I've let you..."

"I know. And I'm glad."

"But," she said, "to tell the truth, I feel afraid again."

"I understand," he said gently. "Perhaps you are worried, now that we have become friends, that I, too, will abandon you."

"Yes," she said in a voice he could barely hear.

"I won't abandon you," he promised.

Nothing was said for several moments. Perhaps the silence made her uncomfortable, or perhaps in an attempt to regain her composure, she asked, "Did I ever tell you what happened to Tullio?"

"No, but I have been wondering." He sat and leaned back against her trunk.

Was it his imagination, or did he feel one of her lower branches move down and nestle against his shoulder?

Chapter Ten

"**A**s I told you," she continued, "after the family left the house, no one ever returned. Well, that's not exactly true. Tullio returned."

He knew this, of course, because he had met Tullio several days before.

"When Tullio left, he was a boy of fourteen. He was strong, handsome and, most importantly, he was a good boy.

"The day he left was, I think, the saddest day of my life. And it was...until the day he returned. You see, I didn't know that Tullio's family was leaving for good. But days turned into weeks, and weeks turned into months, and months turned into years. Sometimes, your mind plays tricks on you and I always thought that if I were ever to see Tullio again, he would come back to me as if he were still fourteen, and we would continue our life together, just like before. That hope kept me alive for many years. But, of course, it was not to be."

"Sometimes our hopes can be so disappointing," Rob said softly.

"One day, about fifty years ago, I watched as a car approached the house. A man was being helped out of the car by a woman in a nurse's uniform. When they were both out of the car, I noticed that the man was being pushed up the driveway in a wheelchair. I said nothing and remained very still. I was embarrassed by my appearance, but by then I had lost all interest in everyone and everything."

"You had given up all hope," he said.

"Yes," and she removed her branch from his shoulder.

"Please," he said, "go on."

"As the man in the wheelchair approached, I was overcome with feelings. He seemed familiar, but then again, he didn't. He was not old, but he had the gaunt, hollow look of a much older man. There was no life in his face. And then I heard him speak, and at once my heart was both exhilarated...and broken."

"The man was Tullio," Rob said quietly, "not as you imagined him but as he really was."

"Yes, the man he had become was not the boy I had remembered. Not the Tullio I had waited for. Tullio had spent the last year of the war in a military hospital. He was wounded when the partisans tried to help the villagers of Sant'Anna de Stazzema." The orange tree seemed to wilt before him, as if she were overcome with enormous sadness. "Do you know what happened at Sant'Anna?"

He nodded. The family had driven there a few days before and had seen the little church where the men, women and children of all the surrounding villages were assembled, lined up against the wall, and massacred by the Nazis.

"Tullio's regiment tried in vain to prevent the slaughter, and it was there that Tullio fell—my sweet, innocent Tullio."

"How did you find all this out?" he asked.

"Why, from Tullio himself. He would come and sit by me, over the years, and talk to me. Actually, he would talk to himself and I would listen, for I never revealed myself to anyone before you."

"Never before? In all these years? Not even Tullio? I am very honored...and very grateful," he said. "Tell me more...please."

"I suffered in silence," she went on, "as I contemplated the cruelty imposed upon my poor Tullio. It was then I decided that I wanted no part of this world."

"But Tullio did come back to you. Tullio never really abandoned you. And I see you are able to bear fruit again, even though..."

"I know, I know," she interrupted, "even though it's bitter. But that's because of the way I experienced the world after Tullio came back. And though Tullio comes to visit me from time to time, it's not the same. *He's* not the same. I am always grateful for his company, of course, but I am also a little sad. Not so much because he leaves me, but because I am reminded that life can be so...so..."

"Bittersweet?" he suggested.

"Well, let's just say that it's been a long time since I have known the second part of that word."

How his heart reached out to her. He wanted to reassure her that if...no, when he bought this house, he would never leave her. He would water her and trim her boughs, as carefully as Tullio once did, taking care never to hurt her. He would protect her from the winter's cold. She would have a new family, for generations to come, who would love and protect her, feed her, and eat the sweetest of oranges from her branches.

He told her all that, and more.

And this time there was no mistaking it when he felt not one, but two, of her branches reach down and embrace him.

Chapter Eleven

"Dad, Dad, wake up!" Jesse said, his arms wrapped around Rob's shoulders. "Mom and I were up at the *frantoio* learning all about how olive oil is made."

"Huh?" he said drowsily, rubbing his eyes. "I...I must have fallen asleep. I was having such an unusual...dream. What time is it?" The world slowly was coming back into focus.

"It's four o'clock, honey," Karen responded. "We really should get going. The stores are just reopening and we have to do some shopping before dinner."

"Right...right," he said, "and I've got to make some calls about this house, find out who owns it and if it's for sale. He yawned and stretched. "There's something very special about this house, don't you think?"

"I love it," Karen said.

"Me too," added Jesse.

Rob stood and reached into his pocket for the car keys. And yes, the orange was there. He glanced back at the house, at the olive trees...and at the beautiful orange tree.

When they arrived at the bottom of the driveway, he took the orange out of his pocket. He peeled it, and offered sections to Karen and Jesse.

"Mmmmmm, delicious," they both exclaimed. "So sweet."

It has been five years since that day, the day Rob fell asleep under the old orange tree. So much has happened since then. They did buy the old house. Rob, Karen and Jesse spent over a year restoring it. They furnished it with beautiful antiques and built a large *terrazza* with a magnificent *pergola* covered with grapevines, where they often enjoy meals and savor the sea breezes that come up through the valley. They brought back love, warmth and a child's laughter to the old house.

Tullio's orange tree has since become Jesse's tree. Jesse takes care of her, making sure she gets all the special love and attention that Tullio once gave. She has regained her prominence as the finest of orange trees. Her oranges are plentiful and delicious, and she gives off the sweetest perfume in the hills. Not a day goes by that the family doesn't appreciate her. And she seems to know it.

Tullio passed away last year, but not before he brought the olive trees back to life. Each year he would come to clean the land and prune the olive trees. He would lay the netting down to collect the dropping olives and then gently stroke the tops of the trees with a broom to gather the rest. He would take the olives to the local *frantoio* to be pressed into the finest oil.

He was buried in the old church cemetery, just above his beloved olive trees, where he could still keep a watchful eye on the land.

That is the end of the story. But if you ever find yourself in the hills of Tuscany, in the village of Pieve a Elici, go up to San Pantaleone and look down at the old house. You will know it, because amid the hundreds of olive trees, snuggling against the house so high that one can reach out the third story window to pick her oranges, stands the finest, proudest, most loved orange tree in all of Pieve a Elici. If not the whole world.

The End